Back to Bed, Ed!

by Sebastien Braun

HarperCollins *Children's Books*

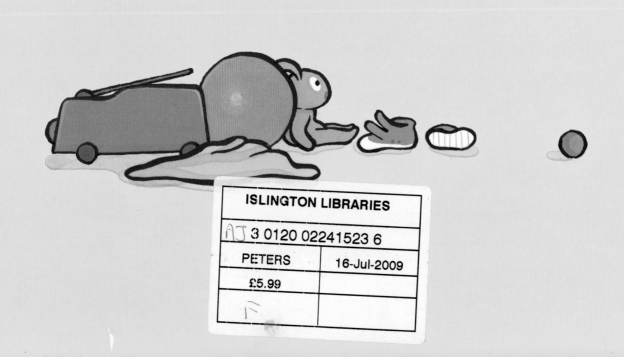

Every night Ed loved getting ready for bed.

He played games with Dad,

clop
clip

he had a drink,

Sip sip

he cleaned his teeth.

Brush
Brush

He had a wash in the bath,

Splish Splash

a story with Mum,

then, all tucked up in bed,

Kiss Kiss Night Night

sleep tight!

Click

Ed LOVED
going to bed...

but Ed **HATED** staying in bed...

Tip toe tip toe...

'Dad! It's too dark in my room.'

'Back to bed, Ed!' grunted Dad.

But Ed didn't go back to his bed,

and Dad didn't get much sleep that night.

The next morning Dad said,

'Stay in your own
bed, Ed!

You're a
BiG mouse
now!'

But later that night,

Tip toe
Tip toe

'Mum! There are MONSTERS in my bedroom!'

'Back to bed, Ed!' groaned Mum.

But Ed didn't go back to his bed.
Mum and Dad didn't get much sleep that night.

The next morning they slept through the alarm.
Dad was late for work.

Ed was late for nursery.

And so it went on, night after night Ed left his bed.

Mum!
Dad!

Mum! Mum!

Dad! Dad!

MUM!
DAD!

'Back to
Bed, Ed!'

they shouted.

Mum and Dad had had enough!

The next morning they came up with a plan...

That night when Ed went to Mum and Dad's bedroom,
the door was shut. He couldn't go in.

Poor Ed didn't know what to do.

Sniff
Sniff
Sniff

Dad came out.
'Come on Ed, back to bed!' he said.

'The night light is on,
you've got your friend.
Stay in your own bed.
You're a big mouse now.'

But Ed didn't stay in bed. He got up and found

 his ted,

 his frog,

his squirrel.

 his duck,

Now he had *all*
his little friends
around him.

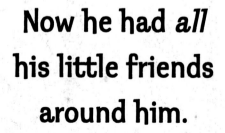

'There's no need
to be scared,'
he said,
'I'm here now.'

After that Ed always slept in his own bed,

and everyone got
a good night's sleep...

Well, not quite everyone!

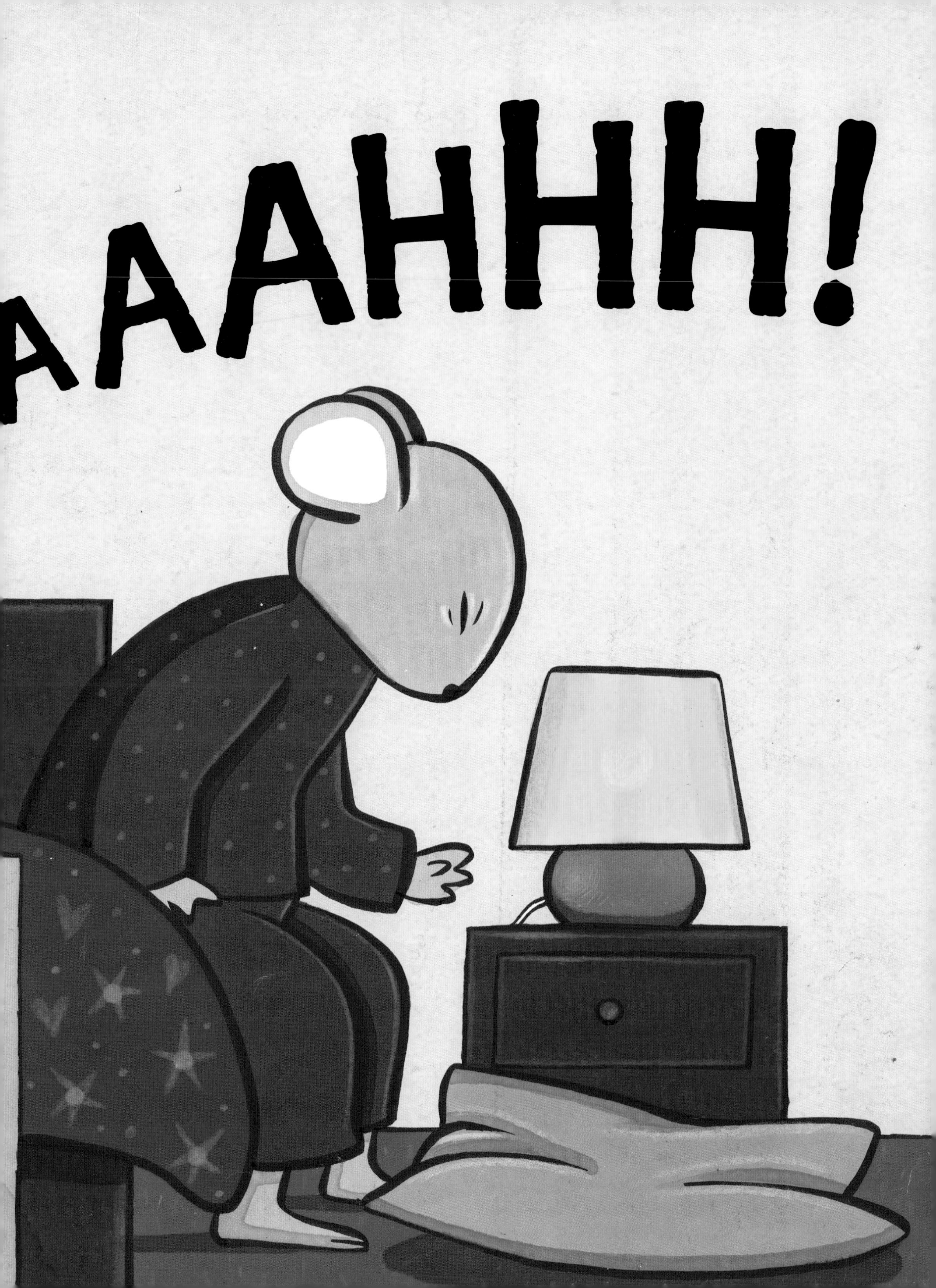
AAAHHH!

Sleep tight, Ed!